Humpfree Gooseoff and More

Darla Pigeon

ISBN: 9798655425101

DEDICATION

To my grandchildren and great grandchildren, may they always enjoy reading and learning. I hope they learn to write silly, adventures, and humorous stories. Write often and share your stories. Keep writing!

CONTENTS

ACKNOWLEDGMENTS

To all those that have listened to my silly stories thru the years I thank you. To my neighbor for supporting me thru the process and is always willing to help, Thank you Don for everything. Thank you to Len Watson for allowing me to use his story from LIR.

1. ANCIENT ONE

In the deep woods, of a long ago forgotten forest, in the Northern woods of New Hampshire I walked alone. I walk thinking about what I should be doing with my life. I know that being alone to think in nature and to hear what the animals have to say will help me. Then I see before me a blanket of mist rising slowly from the ground. I walked into the mist that engulfed me like a robe. The mist caressed my face and body, holding me tight. There is much color, like the colors of the rainbow. This mist makes me feel safe and loved; it lifts me and guides me. Suddenly the mist leaves me and I find myself in a meadow with bright flowers all around. A rainbow graces the sky with bright sunlight.

An old man is waiting for me. His white hair brushes his shoulders; tall slender with a narrow face whose jaw comes to a point. His hair is like a horse's tail, feathery and thick. The old Indian man wears the claws of a bear for a necklace and a bluish purple stone decorates the necklace between the bear claws. The old man's eyes burn with fire but I am not afraid. He opens his hands and offers me a ball of love. I know this because he tells me what the ball is. The love glows like the color of maple syrup. I now realize that this is one of the ancient ones that my people talk about. So I take the ball, feeling the love flow through me, it engulfs my whole being. The love renews me giving me strength.

Creator will not interfere on this side of the veil. Man must learn to live as brothers and sisters or perish on their own accord. The ancient one is able to cross the thin veil that separates our two worlds, the veil side where our ancestors reside and Creator is all powerful.

I hand back the ball of love to the ancient one and it turns into wampum. The wampum has been formed in intricate designs. The ancient one teaches me how to read the meanings of shell life. The meaning of all living things are important to my people, so I am excited to learn what he has to teach me. He speaks thru his mind touching my mind. It is like hearing a voice when no one has spoken.

The ancient one tells me that I was an interpreter before I was born to this world. I am expected to carry the same duties out here on earth, no matter if people think I am strange. Because to them I will be, the ancient ways are not for all people. He says that I must help others from both sides of the veil. The bear knows all of the happenings on earth. Let the people know the bear is coming to dance with them.

The ancient one says I must pray for leadership that I will need in this new world I am in. May you encompass all Creator has placed on your shoulders as you walk thru this life. You must now guide all those who come to you, make their path as sacred as you can. Make their journey home swift, as when they first ran. Teach them to not fear the unknown. Their journey will be short and then they will be home, to rejoin all those that have gone on before them.

Your ancestors walk with you now and always. You must watch the signs that nature sends to you, their meanings mean more than you think sometimes. May you spend time in prayer and meditation, to bring peace to your inner self. Above all things, know that I will walk with you now and always. If you need me you must only call me.

The ancient one sits on a log from a downed maple tree, he is very quiet. Soon the animals emerge from the forest and watch him. The old man touches them with his mind, but the animals do not fear him. The ancient one explains the journey that I am on and asks them if they will help guide me. Telling them my knowledge to communicate is great, that I will be able to understand them. But they must show patience with me, so that I will totally understand their meaning.

The animals tell the old man they must call for the bear to hold a council meeting. Then they will decide. The rabbit tells the old man to come back in five days to hear the answer. The old man agrees and asks if he may speak at the council meeting. The rabbit tells him that it is up to the bear, as he is the chief. I will come and tell you the answer in one day's time.

The rabbit sends the message to bear about having a council meeting and that the ancient one wants to speak before the council. Rabbit tells the other animals about his message and they all wait to hear if bear will call a council meeting.

Soon the deer brings the word that there will be a council meeting and bear will allow the ancient one to speak. Bear sends word to all the animals that the ancient one will speak at the council meeting. Bear tells the animals that when the ancient one is done they will all discuss what has been said. Then a decision will be made. The animals all feel that this is fair and the most honest way to do it. They are sure that bears wisdom in handling this will make things better for all.

Rabbit goes to tell the ancient one the decision about the council meeting and that he will be allowed to speak. The ancient one agrees that he will be at the council meeting and will accept the decision of the council.

The animals have all gathered for the council meeting. There is much chatter going on between the animals about what the ancient one will have to say. They wonder if he too has the wisdom which bear has. They chatter so much and so loudly, that bear has to growl real loud to bring the meeting to order.

The ancient one arrives and bear calls the meeting to order. Bear once more tells all the animals that they must listen and take in what the ancient one has to say with an open heart.

The ancient one stands to speak. I know that man has not always lived by the laws of your people nor have they lived by the laws of Mother Earth. He pauses to see what the animal's reaction will be. The animals look wide eyed as no man has come before them and ever admitted that their people have done wrong.

The ancient one takes a deep breath and slowly lets it out. Once again he starts to talk telling them of this special one that can hear them and understand them. They will be able to guide this new person and nurture them in their ways. But this can only happen if both parties, the animals and human, interact with true faith. One without the other is no good to man or animals. The world is deteriorating and can only be fixed if people are willing to learn what has to be done. You must teach this human what must happen to restore our world and hold true all of our beliefs. This will give true peace to man and animals alike to be able to live together without hurting each other. Then he pauses from his talk and looks up to the heavens and all the animals bow their heads knowing he is praying for understanding.

Then he says that he can't tell them what to do but I hope you will consider what I have said. I must go now and wait your decision, may peace be with all of you and may creator guide you in your decision.

The animals looked around at each other, except for the skunks. The eldest skunk said what a schmuck to talk to us like that.

The rest of the animals sat silently looking at bear. Bear lowered his head in prayer and the other animals followed his lead. When he was done with his prayer, he brought his head up and cleared his throat; bear said we must consider what the ancient one has presented to us. We must consider all of what has been said, with a clear mind and no prejudice or we to will be acting like man. A clear mind and a clear heart will bring forth the truth of what we should do. Remember we to must live in this world and like man must survive together. The ancient one has presented us with a way to communicate to man. Our world is deteriorating and with it comes extinction of all living things. All that will remain is a dead world. Is this what we pray for?

Open your hearts and think about what you truly want to happen to our world. Don't misjudge what has been said until you have time to think about it. Go now and think about what has been said here. We will meet in three days to make a decision about how we will handle this matter.

Three days passed the animals talked with one another. Their families considered what would happen if the decision was made one way or the other.

All the animals agreed that bear was the wisest of all the animals. What bear had said to them was very powerful. It moved the emotions of the animals in a way no one ever thought they could be swayed. Life and death of their world was powerful. But could this person the ancient one spoke off really be able to make man see that they were destroying their world? The animals were not sure that they could trust this to happen.

Time was up, today was to be the meeting. The animals went to the meeting still unsure of what they would say or do.

As always bear started the meeting with a prayer for both guidance and the wisdom to do what was right. To allow that wisdom to flow through the other animals so they too might make the right choice. Bear lifted his head. He asked who would speak first. The elder skunk said that he would. Once again the skunk would call the ancient one a schmuck. Bear roared with anger. What have I said about having an open mind? You may leave our council if you cannot show respect to one who has spoken before us. I didn't ask you to love him or to agree with him but I do know you must show respect for him. Respect is something that must be shown to all things. If you don't wish to observe our laws you may leave. The skunk says you are right bear. I have already said too much, your wisdom is what we should follow. All the other animals agreed. So a vote was taken and the meeting was over. Bear would talk to the ancient one later in the day.

Later that day bear met with the ancient one and told him of the animal's decision. Bear states that the animals are still leery of this special one. The animals have agreed to try and help this one to understand all that needs to be learned.

The ancient one says the special one will be called Maho but let it be known now that Maho can only do so much. Maho's job is to go out in the world and try to teach man what the animals have taught him. Sometimes he will need to call on the animals for guidance. So word must be sent out to all the animals so they will know to help him when he needs it.

Bear agrees that this will be done. Bear and the ancient one say their goodbyes.

The ancient one must now go back to talk to the special one. The special one greets the ancient one as he arrives back at the old maple log. They sit to talk and the ancient one says you will be called Maho from this day forward and for the rest of your days. The animals have agreed to teach you. So go now and learn the ways of this big beautiful world we live in. Remember I am only a prayer away, you may call of me anytime that you need me. Go my friend, peace be with you. May Creator grant you all the help you need on your journey through life.

So Maho council's with the animals, then goes out in the world to spread the word of how man can save his world and the animals. His message is respect. Respect for all things great and small.

Maho's message to this day has not totally been received by man. Today we see climate change, pollution along our roadsides, rivers, lakes and ponds. When will man learn not to kill his own environment?

2 THE GREATEST MOUNTAIN MAN

Gabe LaPlay was born on Mount Evans in the state of Colorado. He was born in a small cabin his father had built many years ago. The cabin had a dirt floor, log walls that were filled with clay and a moss roof. You see the cabin was built into the mountain under a ledge.

Gabe was born on a very cold cloudy day when his father was away hunting for game to feed them thru the winter. During this time of year his father was often gone for many days at a time.

Gabe's mother was used to being alone. But this was her first child and she was really very nervous about the birth. There was no close neighbors but one of the Indian women they had met said she would stop in each day till the baby came. Gabe's mother had prepared everything a head of time so when the baby came during the night she was prepared. Everything went well with the birth.

Gabe weighed in at eight to nine pounds was his mothers guess. He had a head of hair and was always hungry but he did sleep well at night.

The baby grew fast and by spring he was crawling and trying to walk.

Spring was a time when the snow was leaving the mountain top. You could tell spring was here the streams became larger and ran more swiftly. But it was also a time of danger; you could have mudslides that would also cause rock slides.

During the spring his father hunted for beaver. The furs that his father had collected thru the winter and beaver pelts would trade for food and other supplies.

Trapping and hunting was an everyday thing but it also was dangerous on the mountains. Cougar, Coyote and Black Bear were the most dangerous of all.

Mount Maroon Bells and Mount Evans were the most dangerous areas to hunt and trap on. Rattlesnakes were plentiful on the mountains and sometimes there was no warning when they were going to strike.

Gabe is growing up and his mother has had two more children. His brothers Landon and Emmett were younger than him but almost the same size. All the boys had learned to hunt and fish.

It has been a poor year so is father is going to travel to Pike's Pike. Climbing the mountain is a feat in itself let alone the fact that your body has to adjust to the elevation and thinnest of the air at that height. The animals aren't as plentiful but his father has had some luck on that mountain. The last time his father was there he trapped jackalope and snow hare. His father also got to shot two big horn sheep. The trapping and hunting is very important for food and clothing. The children were growing bigger all the time.

The indigenous people are all around us and more noticeable. They used to keep their distance from us but now they wish to trade with us. The Puebloan people live in the valley and up on the mesa. Apache people are living on the plains along with the Comanche who live up in the high plains.

The Cheyenne are living near the Rocky Mountains but each wants to trade different things. But even with all these tribes around the Ute's in the 1880's controlled most of Colorado.

All the miners and fur traders were thought to be very friendly with the Indians. During this time more and more settlers came to make their homes. This caused a lot of trouble with the natives. They were killing the animals for sport and that affected the Indians way of life. It caused a shortage of food for them and also for the trappers that had come a long time ago. Like Gabe's father. The natives did not believe in hunting for the fun of it. The war was going to come soon if this continued.

Gabe had learned much about hunting, trapping, survival skills and how to ride a horse. So the day the army came to town looking for men to join the army. Gabe was going to sign up as he had just turned eighteen. He became an army scout because he knew the area so well. During that time the Indians were at war with Mexico.

Gabe was friends with Chief Ourey and his wife Chipita from the Ute nation. The chiefs' wife had made Gabe a beaded knife belt. Gabe was like a son to them, as they never had any children. Many years ago Gabe's father had brought him to the camp to trade furs. Chipita had fallen for the boy then. Gabe had fallen asleep in her arms while playing with the beads around her neck.

The chief gave him information about what was going on in the area which was very helpful to the soldiers.

Gabe was allowed to dress like the Indians as it made it easier for him to travel into their camps. Most of the Indians resented the soldiers. So Gabe dressed in his buckskin leggings and deer skin over shirt. He often wore moccasins and a fur beaver cap that had been given to him by his father. He carried a powder horn with a bullet pouch for balls and a flint. His gun was kept out of sight under his shirt. The other soldiers thought he was strange because of the way he dressed. They didn't understand that he was going into Indian encampments alone.

They sat around the campfire many a night listening to the older soldiers tell about the battles they had been in and the women they had been with. Many tales of duty stations they had been at. They told about officers and how many of them had ugly wives. This really wasn't true but many of the stories they told were made up

Now Gabe he could tell some real whoppers of a story. For you see mountain men that scouted for the army had a lot of free time on their hands. For you see when the days grew dark and the streams froze over there was little to do but tell stories. Mountain men proudly claimed to be the inventors of tall tales.

Gabe was one of the best tall tales tellers for he was young and had a good imagination for making up tales of things he had seen. So now we will learn a few of the tales he told.

Gabe was busy telling the fellows about the time he came upon this powerful water spout. Gabe described the thing as hissing something terrific like a snake that was about to strike. The thing spouted water more than seventy feet in the air.   Then it would be silent for a long time and then it would attack without warning.

He told of the hot springs that were hot enough for cooking. He told of how it would burn you and that it smelled so pungent. So the other soldiers would ask why would you want to cook where it smell so bad. Gabe would reply because how else would you warm your food with no wood around.

Gabe told of the large brown hairy monsters that came to drink and sometimes in the winter would be covered by frozen snow, so much you thought the snow was walking around. He told how the monsters could creep up on you without you knowing it and once the monster had sent him flying in the air at least fifty feet. He told how the monster stood on his hind legs and was able to walk towards him. Growling the terrible frightening sound and how his claws were long and sharp as a razor.

Gabe had once seen what this monster did to a tree the marks on the tree were deep and long. Gabe told about seeing the monster sitting on the ground with his legs wrapped around a bush of berries just raking them fistful after fistful.

Gabe told of the buffalo he had experienced. He had seen the wonders of this magnificent creature. The buffalo must have weighed ten times what a grown man would weigh or maybe more. That would have been the smaller ones. The buffalo ran very fast for their size and would charge a human.

Gabe's stories were about the Yellowstone Valley that he had traveled through during his teenage years.

Gabe told the story of how he received his name. Well, the story goes like this. Gabe was but a young boy learning to hunt for the first time but his father told him not to tell the other men it was his first time because they would not let him hunt with them.

Gabe was hunting with the men on a nice clear but crisp winter day in the snow packed forest of oak trees when he saw a mighty fine elk. The elk was grazing peacefully and paying him no mine. Gabe raised his rifle and fired, Kaboom! Kaboom! He missed the fine elk he was shooting at and the older men laughed. They thought he was playing with them by missing so they called him Gabe play and because he was French they added the La to make his name LaPlay. This was a great story and Gabe loved to tell this tale about his name even though he knew it wasn't true.

3 THE WOODS

Far into the woods nestled under the snowcap mountains, near a long winding river, where the water rushes over the stones, hurrying on its way to another place. Spruce, Elm and Pine trees stand all about. The pine smell is never far from your nostrils. Yet you still can see wildflowers standing in the open field.

Across the way lies a twenty-room motel painted white with red trim. Small blue diner sits next door, with the smell of bacon wafting across the road. I'm hungry from just the smell of the bacon.

Fragrance of Lilacs is consumed by everything. Flowers are not fully in bloom, yet they are rich in beauty. First buds blooming sending sweet scent of lilac in the air. I never imagined a lilac bush growing right out of a riverbank. Right there a month ago or more was solid ice. Now stands a lovely fragrant bush.

I sit on the soft brown pine needles, watching hummingbirds come to the flowers. They taste the juices of the sweet scented flower. Hummingbird small wings flitter and flutter like a fast moving fan. Yet he drinks from the flower, and then quickly moves on. In the background I hear the pecking of a very large woodpecker as he looks for insects in and old dead tree.

Pine trees stand so tall the light diminished but still I notice the sun is going down in the west along the horizon. The large pine trees will hide some of the stars at night.

Smoke is rising from the campfire. I can smell the wood fire and hear the sizzling of hamburgers cooking. The air is full of the smell of fresh dirt that has been cleared near the fire for everyone to sit.

Supper is ready and the juicy hamburger tastes better than anything I have eaten. Juices run from mine, soaking the bread with its fine juices. I watch the stars come out as I am eating.

A twinkle here then another, soon the sky is full of stars. I lay on my back watching the stars, trying to find the big dipper. Then I see an animal, a great big fat dinosaur, so large he fills the sky. Will the stars move on or just stay in the same place? It is then that I think about a lesson I had in school about the seasons changing with the rotation of the Earth. The stars move with the change.

Pine tickles my nostrils while the dew is starting to fall like little fairies. Dew is dropping small water droplets from the sky. Soon I'm snuggled down dreaming of my dinosaur and the place in the sky in which my dinosaur will travel.

I awake as dawn is breaking with the first light of day coming thru the trees. Rays of sun light are playing off the droplets of moisture. Moisture rises like smoke first it is cloudy then you can see it clearly. The dew is rising up beyond the mountains. The dew makes my face wet from its gentle touch. The air is bringing all that dewy moisture to my lips. A small breeze brings the scent of pine and washes it away with a quick swoop.

Light breeze travels through the trees rushing on. Telling the birds to wake up for I must move on. Birds sing their songs flying here and there. Birds are finding things to eat. A Robin flies by with a small stick in its mouth. Sparrows have dried grass from last year. They are building their nest for their young.

Soon the sun will come out and warm everything up. The animals in the forest are starting to stir.

I see a deer down by the lake having a drink of water. A fish jumps out of the water scaring the deer away. The fish are active today jumping to and fro after the insects flying just above the water.

A beaver swims by and then suddenly starts to bang his tail on the water. Sending a message that humans are near. Beware as you swim along.

The sun glistens off the lake. As I sit to paint by the lake I see geese coming in for a landing. They squawk very loudly and all of a sudden they have landed in the water. They land smoothly just a small ripple of the water.

I paint pictures of the geese and the trees in the background. But to soon the sun is going down and I must return home. I have to go to work tomorrow. So I say good-bye to the lake, woods and wildlife. I will come back soon.

4. Bad Days for a Bear

My name is Ant. I was born in February in the great White Mountains of New Hampshire. I was born in a den, under a rock crevice. I have a brother who is really into doing all of the activities that mother does. I think he maybe a perfect bear.

I'm a little mischievous. Right now my mother is growling at me with displeasure. I guess she doesn't understand me. I want to play and investigate my surroundings. There is plenty of time to learn other things.

I got my name around April. We were walking along this well traveled path by the Lost River. I was looking for something to do, when I soon spotted this large hill. Reaching my paw into the hole in the hill, I pulled out these funny red creatures. My paw was covered with so many of these things that I couldn't see my paw anymore. I decided to eat these small funny red creatures, and they are quite good. Then all of a sudden

the red ants started to bite my nose. This was not funny.
I was not a very happy bear now, so I went running to
mother for help.

Mother shook her head. "You will learn and I shall
name you Ant," said mother. So that is how I got my
name.

So Ant I am. Come with me thru the forest of dark
green leaves. The forest floor smells of sweet damp
earth. New buds with bright green leaves are growing on
the trees. Flowers are all around just pocking their heads
from the earth. The sun is shining brighter each day
making the earth warm for a bear to roll around. Spring
has arrived a good time for eating. I like to eat all the
time.

We are busy eating grasses that are new and just
coming from the ground. The plants that are just poking
their heads from the earth are tender and juicy. My belly
is very full from eating these.

Mother tells us many things about where to find good
berries, grubs, mice and other small insects to eat.
Mother has told us how to find water. Mother says, "You
must leave the older bears alone and never try to take
anyone's food, because that will cause a big fight."

Mother and brother is busy turning over rocks and
logs. They are searching for those fat juicy grubs. They

eat whatever they find, sometimes insects or mice, but the juicy grubs are the best. I have eaten enough to make my belly swell.

I decide it would be much more fun to run over and tackle my brother. Which I immediately do! Wrestling my brother to the ground and we roll down a small hill, rustling through the old leaves. Twigs break underneath us but still we roll on. Then THUD! My head hits this large white rock. My head hurts and I see stars. Brother rushes away, back to where mother is standing. I turn my head to look at the rock. Deciding I can't eat the rock, I move on.

I am standing on my hind paws to see what I can see; when my brother attacks me from behind sending me flying. We roll over and over again finally stopping against something that looks like a tree taking a nap. I stick my head into the end, and smell a sweet scent. Feeling hungry I push my head farther into the hole. Finding nothing to my liking, I try to pull my head out, but I can't. My head is stuck. Oh! What will I do now?

Standing up seemed like a good idea, but to stand with a tree on your head isn't easy. Swaying one way then the other way suddenly falling backwards I hit the ground hard. CRACK! The tree falls away from my head. I stand looking around to see if mother saw what happened. Oh! good she is busy eating, not watching me. I rush back to mother's side. I hurt so much I lay down on the soft green grass. I fall asleep watching the trees sway in the soft warm air. The wind rustling thru the leaves lulls me to sleep. Soon mother wakes me we're on the move again.

I wake to another day. It is very warm. I'm walking along when I spot these funny little green things with long back legs. They jump from one blade of grass to another. I watch them with a great desire to jump like them. I finally try jumping like them by springing from my back legs just like the creature does, but I fall on my head. I try again and again, still falling on my head each and every time.

"They are grasshoppers and you are a black bear, you are supposed to eat them," Mother says. So now I try to catch them to eat but they are very fast. I spend many days trying to catch them before I get fast enough. But soon they fill my belly to the top.

Right before my eyes is this yellow and black striped buzzing creature. Making his wings go so fast you would think he would fall to the ground from working so hard. I watch as they fly away up into the tree. I hear the buzzing….buzz….buzz….and soon I realize that these are honey bees that mother told us about. Up in the tree, I climb up into the tree for honey.

Honey is what bears like best. Sticking my head in the hole I get my big black nose full of honey. I pull my head from the hole, stick my paw in and pull out some honey. While I'm licking honey from my paw, the bees sting my nose. I swat them and eat them too. Bees are a little crunchy, but good for a growing bear like me. Bees were swarming all around me. The bees make my fur move so I know they are there. But they can't hurt me. When I reach my paw back in to get some more honey, I slip and fall from the tree but not before getting a paw full of honey.

Oh! What a great day it has been to be a bear!

Many days of adventures I have enjoyed in the last eighteen months. Many things I have learnt.

I am washing down by the river, rolling in the mud to wash the bugs from my fur, I realize that soon these lazy days will be over and brother and I will be all alone.

Mother has tried to teach us all we need to know. The lessons mother taught us will help us the rest of our lives even though we didn't know that then. Brother was a good bear. But I also learned what mother was teaching. I just had a few other adventures.

Well brother and I are off to hibernate. We will stay together till mating season next year. Then we will live a life of solitude except during two months of mating season. I'm off to have more adventures, wish you could join me.

5. HUMPFREE GOOSEOFF

Francis pressed his face against the window pane. He looked out at all the tall buildings, wondering how kindergarten would be. Francis and his family had just moved to the city and he had not made any friends yet. That made him very sad.

Just then Francis heard a noise in his closet. Francis opened the door to his closet very carefully, one day after hearing a scratching sound, thinking it was a mouse. As he opened the closet he saw this very large thing which was purple with yellow. Francis quickly slammed the closet door shut. Leaning against it to make sure whatever it was it didn't get out. Francis opens the door again, just to see if the thing was still there. Sure enough it was still there.

Francis said, "Do you talk and what are you?"

The thing said, "My name is Humpfree Gooseoff.

Francis said, "What is a Humpfree Goose.

The thing said, "Humpfree Gooseoff is not what I

am." "I am a dragon from a land far away", said the dragon. "You may call me Humpfree or Goose", the dragon tells Francis.

Francis replied, "I will call you Humpfree."

Humpfree steps out of the closet banging his head on the door. "Ouch!" said Humpfree. Then a small puff of smoke rises from the dragon's nostril.

Francis hollers, "Don't burn the house down." Just at that moment the dragon swings his tail around and all the toys flew across the room.

"Oh my! What will I do with you," said Francis. "You will either burn the house down or destroy it with your tail." Francis tells Humpfree.

"I'm sorry," said the dragon. I just need more room. Francis tells the dragon to go back in the closet while he thinks about what to do. The dragon steps back into the closet. Francis tells the dragon he would see him tomorrow morning as he closes the door.

Francis's parents have told him no pets, what would they do if they find out he has a dragon? What will he feed this dragon? What will he do about the dragon's tail and the fire?

The next morning Francis goes to the closet still very worried that he doesn't know much about dragons. Humpfree and Francis sit and talk about the things that are bothering Francis, but the dragon doesn't have the answers.

Francis so wants to have Humpfree for a friend. He has been so lonesome since the move to the city. Francis sits with his elbows on his knees holding his head.

"What am I to do Humpfree if I keep you my parents will be mad and make you go away," said Francis.

The dragon tells him he doesn't have the answer but will go away if that is what he wants. Humpfree is tired so back in the closet he goes to sleep.

Francis tells Humpfree he will try to find an answer before tomorrow.

The next morning Francis was having breakfast and decides to ask Mrs. Wells where she would play with a very large animal like a dragon.

Mrs. Wells laughs and said, "If I had a dragon I would take him to play in the park down the street."

Francis asks if they will be able to go to the park later. Mrs. Wells said, "Yes of course."

Francis asks the dragon." how will I get you to the park without Mrs. Wells knowing".

Humpfree tells Francis that he will be invisible. Several weeks go by, the dragon had no problem moving his tail or blowing puffs of smoke in the park.

Francis and Humpfree were playing by a large oak tree, Humpfree had flown up on to the limb above were Francis was lying on the grass. Humpfree was telling Francis what it was like to be a dragon. Suddenly a ball lands on Francis's stomach. Francis was startled, so he sat up looking all around. Francis saw a dark haired boy running towards him.

The boy said, "You found my ball."

"No it hit me in the stomach," said Francis.

"I'm so sorry," said the boy.

Francis asks "what is your name."

"Pedro, "said the boy.

"Mine is Francis would you like to be friends," said Francis.

"Yes", said Pedro.

Many days go by as Francis and Pedro play in the park. They meet other boys their age. Summer is over and school had started, Francis and Pedro are in the same kindergarten class. They spent many hours playing at each other's house.

One day Mrs. Wells asked, "Francis how is your dragon?"

Francis said, "Humpfree has gone to play with another

lonely boy."

"Everyone needs someone to play with," said Mrs. Wells.

6. A Tale of a Tail

Possum had a great bushy tail which he liked to show to everyone. One day at animal council Possum was bragging about his beautiful tail. Possum thought he should be able to speak first because he had the most magnificent tail of all the animals. Possum bragged that his tail was nicer than squirrels and even better than red foxes.

Possum wanted to speak first at the animal council meeting. He was sure that Great Bear would let him. The animals were really tired of hearing Possum brag. They decided to do something about it. What they would do no one was sure of, but something had to be done.

Rabbit was the messenger for the animals. He came to tell each animal that the Great Bear had called for a council meeting for next evening. Along the way Rabbit stopped to see if anyone had any ideas about what to do about Possum.

Rabbit upon seeing Possum noticed his tail was dirty.

Rabbit had an idea. The other animals would be so pleased with him. Rabbit told Possum he had just the stuff to clean his tail. Possum agreed to meet Rabbit at his house that evening.

Rabbit went off to find Snake and ask if he could have one of his old snake skins. Snake was glad to help out Rabbit and gave him the newest one which was larger than all the rest.

Possum arrived and Rabbit went to work placing the potion on Possums' tail. Rabbit then wrapped Possums' tail with the snake skin. Rabbit told Possum not to remove it till the council meeting.

Possum so wanted to groom his tail as this was a daily thing. Sometimes he would groom his tail several times during the day. So all that day Possum was upset but excited, he couldn't wait for the council of animals to meet.

Possum went to sit by Great Bear as council was gathering. He wanted the best seat in the forest. Where he knew all the animals would be looking.

Possum immediately started to brag about his tail. The animals asked him why he had wrapped his tail. Possum said, "I will show you the reason why I wrapped my tail".

Possum ripped off the snake skin. A laugh went through the group of animals. Low and behold all the hair on Possums' tail had fallen off. Possum sneered at the animals as he ran away to hide.

Possum tried to tell himself that the hair would grow back. But days and months went by and the hair had not grown back.

From that day Possum has worn a sneer on his face. His tail is very bald and that's why he only comes out at night.

Have you ever seen a Possum running around at night?

7. SLIPPERS AND A TUTU

When I was very young Grandma would dance in her studio. I would watch and wonder how Grandma danced so well. If it was me I would be worried about dancing so perfect. I couldn't dance in front of people. Grandma said, "stage fright is nothing to worry about and as far as dancing that's what lessons are for." But I was still very worried because I wanted to be a great dancer. What if Grandma wasn't there to help me?

When I was eight I wanted to earn the entertainment patch from Brownies. But I have never danced in front of other people before. Grandma said, "I will come and watch you so just look for me. Don't worry about anything else. You know what you are doing and I will always be there to support you."

Grandma had taught me slow deep breathing exercises to relax me when I was nervous. As I was taking slow deep breaths I realized that it calmed my panic and the butterflies in my stomach went away. I started to dance and found I was getting very nervous, with all the other Brownies watching me. Then I looked for Grandma, she gave me her thumbs up sign, and this relaxed me.

I finished my dance to loud clapping, of all the other Brownies watching me. Everyone thought that it was wonderful that Grandma and I danced.

I wanted so much to dance for my Grandfather, who was unable to come to my recitals, because he was unable to walk do to a car accident.

My other grandparents lived so far away in the State of California. Grandmother Emma would say, "You really have become a wonderful dancer since the last time I saw you."

Then a great opportunity came, a chance to dance in competition, but I wasn't sure I wanted to do it. Grandma said, "You are a wonderful dancer, you probably are the best dancer in the County, not to try out would be a waste of your talent." So I tried out for the County Dance Competition.

I was very nervous back stage when the big day came. I had butterflies in my stomach; I thought I would be sick. I had many reasons to be nervous but mostly because I knew only three could win but twelve would compete. Grandma assured me that I could do it. "Just look for Grandma and not the other people." said Grandma.

My knees shook and I felt them wobble. I had never been this afraid before. I knew Mom, Dad, and Grandma would be watching me but I was still scared I wouldn't be able to dance. What if my feet didn't move?

Running thru Grammas' breathing exercises I relaxed a little. Just before my turn came I looked to see if my parents and Grandma were out there. Reassured that they are in their places, I could relax a little more but my legs were still shaking.

Now it is time to go on stage. The music starts my slippers seem to have wings. They dance away with me; at least that's what I really want to believe. My pink Tutu was beautiful. It reminded me to look for Grandma, as she had made it for me.

There was grandma giving her thumbs up sign which reassured me I was doing well on stage. Before I knew it the routine was over. Now all I had to do was wait. Waiting was the hardest part now.

The announcement was made for third place. A small redhead came to collect her trophy. Then second place was called and another friend who I danced with before claimed her prize. There I stood frozen in place when they called my name. Grandma was standing clapping along with my parents, as I went to collect my trophy and the prize to dance at the Boston Metropolitan Dance Competition.

Now I had a month to get ready to perform in the big show. Just the thought of going to such a big place to perform seemed like light years away on another world. Thinking it was such a long time away I just kept practicing. The time moved so quickly and it was only two days away.

Then the big day arrived. I woke early in the morning so I would have time to practice m routine one more time before leaving. I wanted everything to be perfect.

The phone rings, grandma says, "She can't travel to Boston because she has no one to stay with Grandpa." I run to tell my parents that I can't go without grandma. My parents tell me that I can because I have practiced so hard for this show. "Bianca you will be getting a big surprise in Boston," says Mother.

The show starts I'm nervous, there are thousands of people out there. Mom said, "Dad and I will be in the front row, right in the middle." Mom leaves me to stretch and do my breathing exercises. Things are running through my head. What will I do without Grandma? I have never danced without Grandma being there. Why can't you be here Grandma this time I really need you?

I look to see if everyone is in his place. I dance out on to the stage with Dad videotaping me dancing and right there beside him is Grandma with her thumbs up sign.

What a surprise for me! Both sets of grandparents are there. Grandma Emma has made the long trip from California and that was why Grandma didn't come with us to Boston. She had picked up Grandma Emma at the airport.. But the big surprise was Grandpa had learned to walk again. Just so he would be able to see me dance.

When the show was over I realized that I hadn't been afraid because I didn't have time to think about it in all the excitement.

Grandma was right. STAGE FRIGHT IS NOTHING TO WORRY ABOUT.

8. DON'T SELL THE BONES OF OUR PEOPLE

"Always remember that your father never sold his country. You must always close your ears whenever you are asked to sign a treaty selling your home," said Chief Joseph. My father lays dying as he says these words to me.

Soon I will be the new Chief. I am only thirty-one very young to be a Chief. My name is also Chief Joseph of the Nez Perce Indians. Many questions need to be answered. Can I protect my people from the white settlers? Can we live in Peace? What will become of my people?

I was born in 1840 in the Wallowa Valley. My people call it the Land of the Winding Water. The Wallowa Valley is located in what is now the state of Oregon.

My tribal name is Hin-mah-too-yah-lah-ket or Thunder Rolling in the Mountains. Many people come to me for advice because I am known as the great thinker. I am pretty reserved and not much of a fighter.

The Nez Perce tribe has lived on the land roaming from the Rocky Mountains into Oregon, Washington and

Idaho. Many small bands of Nez Perce live on the land and follow their leaders.

In 1855 our tribe agreed to give a small part of our territory to the Unites States. The government wanted all Nez Perce Chiefs to give up all the land and settle on a reservation. All our Chiefs refused to grant this to the government of the United States.

My father who was still alive tries to talk to the white government. He told them that the land did not belong to us. That the land belonged to the great Creator and that we were only care givers of the land. Our people rest on these lands, many generations of our people. We as a people can't sell the bones of our ancestors.

I became Chief in 1871 and by that time I had become bitter towards the settlers. I complained t the government, "The white men have told lies for each other. They drive off a great many of our cattle. Some white men brand our cattle so that we can't claim them. We have no friends who plead our cause before the white law councils."

In 1875, President Grant issued a proclamation officially opening the Wallowa Valley to white homesteaders. I tried moving my people to another part of the valley, away from the growing settlements. Our people did not want trouble but the settlers seemed to want to cause trouble.

I said, "The government says we own the land. If we owned the land then we own it still, for we never sold it."

In 1877 General Oliver Otis Howard, a Civil War hero, gave me and other non treaty Chiefs thirty days to move from the Wallowa Valley and from their lands. We were to move to the Lapwai Reservation.

"Many of my young men wanted to fight than be driven like dogs from the land where we were born. The country that holds the bones of our ancestors," said Joseph.

Several days later the warriors slipped away to seek revenge. The warriors raided for five days, killing white settlers and burning whatever stood in their way. I realized now war could not be avoided.

I never fought a battle until the morning of June 17, 1877. At the end of the day thirty-three soldiers had been killed. Only two of my people had been wounded. The Battle of White Bird Canyon will enter the military records as one of the army's worst defeats at the hands of the western Indians.

The Nez Perce War lasted through the summer and fall of 1877. My tribe would cover seventeen hundred miles in seventeen weeks. We fought thirteen battles. We either defeated the troops or we fought them to a standstill.

On September 30, 1877 general Miles caught up with us in the foothills of Bear Paw Mountain. The battle lasted five days under driving snow fall. The army brought in twelve-pound cannons to bombard us.

General Howard reached the battlefield on October 4, 1877. A flag of truce was sent by messenger to tell us to give up. The condition of surrender would be that our tribe could return to the Northwest in peace. I surrendered by handing my rifle to General Miles. I, Chief Joseph, believed General Miles or I never would have surrendered.

Washington officials overruled General Miles. The surviving members of my tribe would never be permitted to return to the Nez Perce homeland. We were to be placed in permanent exile in Oklahoma. When I heard this my only comment was, "When will the white man learn to tell the truth?"

In 1879 I traveled to Washington to plead with the government officials. This is my speech to these officials: "I want the white people to understand my people. Some of you think an Indian is a wild animal. This is a great mistake. I will tell you about our people, and then you can judge whether an Indian is a man or not.

"I have carried a heavy load on my back ever since I was a boy. I learned then that we were but a few, while the white men were many, and that we could not hold our own with them. We were like deer. They were like grizzly bears. We had a small country. Their country was very large. We were content to let things remain as the Great Spirit Chief made them. They were not, and would change the rivers and mountains if they did not suit them.

"As for war, I blame my young men and I blame the white men. I blame General Howard for not giving my people time to get their livestock away from Wallowa Valley. I do not acknowledge that he had the right to order me to leave the Wallowa Valley at any time. I deny that either my father or I ever sold the land. It is still our land. It may never again be our home, but my father sleeps there, and I love it as I love my mother. I left there hoping to avoid bloodshed.

"If the white man wants to live in peace with the Indian, he can live in peace. There need be no trouble. Treat all men alike. Give them all the same laws. Give them all an even chance to live and grow. The Great

Spirit Chief made all men. They are all brothers. The earth is the mother of all people, and all people should have equal rights upon it.

"Whenever the white man treats the Indians as they treat each other, then we shall have no more wars. We shall be all alike, brothers of one father and one mother, with one sky above us and one country around us, and one government for all."

Many people like General Miles appealed to the government in my behalf. Finally in 1855 the Nez Perce where allowed to return to the Northwest. Of the four hundred-seventeen people who had surrendered with me, only two hundred-sixty eight were left.

I was sent to the Colville Reservation in Washington State.

I was telling a friend, "I want to go back there to live. My father and mother are buried there."

Chief Joseph died in September 21, 1904 at the age of sixty-four. The reservation doctor reported the cause of death as "a broken heart."

At the funeral ceremony, his nephew Yellow Wolf said, "Joseph is dead, but his words are not dead. His words will live forever."

Are the words Chief Joseph spoke before the white government, not true today?

9. WHERE GOING WHERE?

I asked, "Where are we going?"

"It's a surprise," teased Father

"Pack plenty of warm clothes along with your blanket," said Mother.

Mother is busy packing the car with coolers. Then in goes the brown bags of groceries.

I ask again, "Where are we going?"

Mother replies, "Camping."

"What! There is no way I'm sleeping outside or being in the woods with nothing to do. What do you think I will find to do? What can we possibly see that we can't see here in the city?" I said.

I hate the thought of camping even though I have never been. I can't imagine what I will find out in the woods that would be of any interest to me at all. Parents think that because they had fun doing this that I will to. What do they know anyway?

Father has packed three strange bags that are rolled up in big balls then in goes this metal square box and a round tank of some kind. Throwing in more and more stuff till the car is packed full of stuff. So now we are off on this adventure that Dad things I will enjoy.

We are driving along it seems it like it's been hours. We are now driving along a river following it along this winding road. The river is nestled in amongst the pines. Large Oak trees are all about, with the wind pushing thru the treetops. The river is rushing on, moving swiftly along to another place. Birds are singing in the treetops. Then suddenly a Cardinal rushes by with straw in its beak off to make a nest I guess.

I see pine cones that litter the ground on top of brown discolored needles from the pine trees. It looks like it will make a nice soft bed. The fragrance of pine comes swooping into the car just as we stop along the rushing water. I look up to see white capped mountains and think snow on the mountain when it is warm out.

Birds are singing their songs and calling out to one another. I watch them flutter from one tree limb to another.

Father holler, "come and help unload there is much to do before we can explore."

So mother and I rush over to help unload the car.

Father says," We must put up the tents sleeping under the stars in wonderful but what if it rains."

Mother and I look in disbelief. "You want us to sleep on the ground."

"No," Father says. "We have sleeping bags for you to sleep in."

"Oh!" says mother.

Father says, "Sleeping under the night sky is something to behold."

When camp is setup I am free to explore as long as I am careful and stay near camp. I go over by the pine trees to watch the birds. I sit down on the nice brown pine needles that I soon find are very picky one of the needles stabs me in the leg.   So I move on down by the water to explore the water's edge. I find some little baby fish swimming around. The water seems to be very clear and I can see the bottom under the water.

Father is setting up the square thing with a tank. I find out that it is a stove when I see him place a frying pan on it. Dad is also digging a hole and placing stones around it. So, I wonder up to see what it is.

Father says, "It will be our open fire pit to cook and roast marshmallows in." Dad says, "Find a good strong stick to roast your hot dog on and later you can use it for your marshmallows."

I wander off looking for my stick wondering how I will cook a hot dog without burning the stick up. Well! I think dad must have done this so he will know how.

Night was coming quickly so we started to cook over the open fire with Dad showing both Mother and I how it is done. The hot dogs tasted very different then when we cooked at home. I found that I enjoyed the different taste and wished we would have cooked some more things for me to try.

Now Dad was going to show us how to cook marshmallows over the fire and he had another surprise, Chocolate and graham cookies to add with the marshmallows. We had to cook the marshmallow and then but it and the chocolate between the cookies. Boy was that good and sweet. Boy what a treat!

It was time for bed. The sky was pure black with small twinkling stars, so far away yet so near to me. I lie on my bed roll and look out my tent. I make believe I am drawing characters in the sky. I am making imaginary lines from star to star. I start thinking about writing stories about my wonderful characters in the sky.

Then all of a sudden I hear a rustling noise real close by. What was out there? Would it be large enough to hurt me? I couldn't imagine what it was. The noise continued for what seemed like hours. All of a sudden a small animal sauntered into our camping area over where we had been eating just minutes before. It was looking for food, so I thought I would give it some from our food chest.

I took out some bread and just as I was walking towards the animal.

Dad called out, "no".

I stopped and said, "But the animal is hungry."

Dad said, "Your little friend is a skunk and if you go closer it will spray you."

But Dad,

"No buts about it," Dad Said.

So I went back to my tent. I was very sad and I started to cry. Dad came and talked to me about wild animals. Then I felt much better.

I must have fallen asleep counting the stars; there really were a lot of them.

I awoke to the sun rising, the dew was like a fog, Lifting up towards the snowy mountains. The smell of bacon came waffling to my nostrils from the smoky campfire. Dad was cooking bacon with eggs sizzling in the frying pan.

Dad said, "Soon we will pack to go home, where you like to be."

Then I said, "No Dad I think I like this camping idea of yours."

Dad replied, "So now you like camping after only one night under the stars."

Well I said, "There is so much to explore. I love writing about things I see. I could write a book or fill my journal with all these things."

Dad replied, "Okay I'm sold we will come camping again real soon."

Dad and I laughed because of all the fuss I had put up about going camping and now I liked it.

Mother still wasn't sure if she liked it. Although she said it had some good points. She didn't have to cook. Make beds or do the dishes. But she didn't like sleeping on the ground.

I found out sometimes adventures are fun.

10 FLYING EYES

Mrs. Fox and Bones man lived side by side. Mrs. Fox hunted long hours to find food for her children. She was always looking for a way to make it easier.

Bones man was a skeleton. He had moss and dust hanging from his bones. When he walked he rattled and shook. He could not rest because of a spell placed upon him. Bone man wandered around not knowing what to do.

Mrs. Fox saw Bone man doing something very strange. She stopped to watch what he was doing. Bones man was sitting looking to the East. Then Mrs. Fox saw his eyes fly away. Mrs. Fox stood looking first at Bone man then in the direction of where the eyes had flown.

"Oh! Oh! Oh! Mrs. Fox whispered

She hid behind an oak tree in fear of what magic might be going on. Suddenly like nothing had happened, Bone man's eyes came flying back.

His eyes went right back where they belonged in his eye sockets..

Mrs. Fox was afraid to come out, but thought she must find out why he did this. She slowly approached Bone man.

Bone man looked up. "How are you today?" Bone man asks.

"I am well. I have come to ask you why you send your eyes flying?" said Mrs. Fox.

"I send my eyes looking at the world that I have not seen yet. It was a gift or maybe a curse given to me by the witch. You see I stumbled on the witch when she was doing a spell, on someone and instead of that person having the spell placed on them it was placed on me.

I wish to go see these things, but I cannot." said Bone man. I have a small area to move in only for the remainder of my days. So I send my eyes out to search the world for what I will never be able to go and see.

"Can you give me this curse? It will help me feed my family." said Fox.

Mrs. Fox was asking for this curse but she was not

sure about it at all.

"I will teach you, but you must listen well and follow instructions to the letter," said Bone man.

Bone man tells Fox that she must sit facing the East. You must not move from this position.

"Sing this song 'Ta-Ha-Hey,' when you stop singing your eyes will come back," said Bone man.

Mrs. Fox was worried about this but she knew to feed her family easily this would be a good thing.

Mrs. Fox sat down and began to sing 'Ta-Ha-Hey, Ta-Ha-Hey, Ta-Ha-Hey-------her eyes flew away. She soon saw the great mountains in the East. The great valley below was filled with buffalo, deer, elk and many small animals. She let herself dream of hunting these animals. Mrs. Fox was soon fast asleep. She fell over rolling on the soft grass. She woke jumping to her Feet.

"Oh! Oh! Oh! I have stopped singing. Where are my eyes? What shall I do?" said Mrs. Fox.

Mrs.Fox realized that by moving her eyes must have fallen near her. She knelt down feeling the ground for her eyes. She searched for many hours till she was so tired she needed to sleep.

She woke many hours later hearing her children cry out for her to feed them. So she searched the ground again and found things that were very hard. She placed them her eyes but could see nothing. So she searched again this time she found two things that felt like her eyes. She placed them in her eyes. Mrs. Fox opened her eyes, but everything was yellow. She had placed two gourds in her eyes.

When the children saw her eyes they ran away in fright.

Mrs. Fox searched for many days afraid to leave the spot for fear that she would never find her eyes.

If only she had listened when Bone man told her not to move at all!

Bone man finally stumbled on Mrs. Fox. He said, "What is your problem Mrs. Fox?"

"I have lost my eyes," said Mrs. Fox.

"Well did you move or what happened?" says Bone man.

"I fell asleep dreaming of all the animals that I saw and how I could feed my family for a very long time." said Mrs. Fox

"I will try to help you find your eyes," says Bone man.

Mrs. Fox and Bone man searched for several days not finding anything that was like her eyes. Bone man had never had this happen to him so he was very perplexed as what to do.

So Bone man decided the only way he could help was to send his eyes out in search of the witch. If he found the witch he could send Mrs. Fox to see her for help.

Bone man sat down and started to hum his song and sent his eyes in search of the witch. He had to do this for many a day before he located where the witch was living.

He called for Mrs. Fox to come from her den. When Mrs. Fox came he told her how to find the witch and that she must ask her for a favor to help her find her eyes.

So off Mrs. Fox went in search of the witch. Many time she found herself of the trail that Bone man had told her to take. Everything was so yellow that she sometimes lost her way.

Late one night she heard a voice singing Ta-Ha-Hey over and over again. Mrs. Fox traveled in the direction of the song. Soon she saw the witch and saw that she was collecting something but she couldn't tell what it was.

Mrs. Fox says, "Hello

The witch snaps around and says, "Who are you?"

I am Mrs. Fox she says. I have come to ask you for help.

The witch says; "how may I help you?"

So Mrs. Fox tells her story about how Bone man had taught her what to do and warned her never to move. But that she had fallen asleep.

The witch says, "That is quiet a story my dear but I can help if you don't care who's eyes you get."

"You see I call all the eyes that are wandering or lying around the Earth to come back to me which was what I was doing when you came upon me."

"I will take any eyes but I want to see clearly again," say Mrs. Fox.

"How will you repay me for this deed I will do for you," says the witch.

"What do you want me to do," says Mrs. Fox

The witch thinks about it for several minutes and then she says, "I want you to go and bring Bone man to me," says the witch.

"Are you going to hurt him," says Mrs. Fox

"I have told you what I want will you do it or not," says the witch.

"I will do it but I pray you will not hurt him," says Mrs. Fox.

So the witch gives Mrs. Fox her eyes and reminds her

of her promise to return with Bone man. The witch says, "If you do not return I will call your eyes back to me and then you will be blind forever."

Mrs. Fox sets off for home and to find Bone man. The witch said she removed the spell so he could come to her. It was a long journey and Mrs. Fox wrestled with the fact of bringing Bone man to the witch or losing her eyes. Finally she arrived home.

Bone man was in his usual place. Mrs. Fox told him the story of her adventure and what the witch had demanded for payment.

Bone man said," What more can she do to me? I will go with you to find out what she wants."

So off they go traveling back on the long journey to see the witch. When they arrive the witch greets them.

"Hello my friend you have traveled far and we must eat, so you can travel home again soon," the witch says.

They all sit and eat a wonderful meal. It was like a banquet but Bone man was very nervous about the whole thing. The witch had noticed that Bone man was very nervous.

She said. "Please don't worry about why you are here, it is all good."

Bone man says, "Can we please do whatever it is you

wish to do with me."

The witch says, "Yes, follow me."

Bone man does as he is told and soon the witch is singing over him but he doesn't know why.

Then the witch says, "You are free to go know."

Bone man says, "What did you do to me?"

"Well I set you free from the spell and now you may go anywhere you please but you can no longer send your eyes to see the world," says the witch.

"I have rewarded you for not using the spell to hurt someone else," says the witch.

"Now go my children and do not seek me out again," says the witch.

11. PLANET PLUTO IS A DWARF PLANET

Scientists have decided that Pluto will no longer be a planet. Yet scientists are willing to call Pluto a Dwarf Planet. So is Pluto a planet or not? Some say Yes, because Pluto was considered a planet for 76 years, so why change now? This has become a big controversy even with Pluto's status already having been changed.

Astronomer Clyde Tombaugh discovered Pluto in 1930. Pluto was the ninth planet to be discovered. However in August of 2006 the International Astronomical Union (IAU) demoted Pluto to A Dwarf Planet.

The IAU said that a planet must have three qualities. A planet must have a typical body which orbits the Sun. Planet must be massive enough that its own gravity causes it to form a spherical shape. The planet must have cleared the neighborhood around its orbit.

Pluto meets two of these qualities. Pluto orbits the Sun and is round in shape. However, Pluto has not cleared other objects in its neighborhood.

Pluto's neighborhood is made up by the Kuiper belt. The Kuiper belt which contains nearly a thousand objects including Pluto, Pluto's moon Charon, UB313, asteroid Ceres and Eris which is the largest of these objects.

Pluto is only a faint smudge on the largest telescopes in the world. This has made it hard for scientist to tell what these thousands of objects are. Pluto is merely one of the thousands of objects revolving around the Sun out beyond Neptune.

Many people still want to keep Pluto in the planet family. Astronomers are now considering a way to define planets so that Pluto can once again be a planet. This means many other bodies in the solar system would also qualify to be called planets. This has made the problem even larger than just demoting Pluto. Will Pluto remain a Dwarf Planet? This will not be known till sometime after 2015.

NASA launched the Pluto-Kuiper Belt mission in 2006. It will reach Pluto in 2015 and could possibly explore the Kuiper Belt by 2026.

Do you think if astronomers had found these objects

in the Kuiper belt before they found Pluto; they might not have called Pluto a planet?

Surprises keep popping up in the remotest parts of the solar system. Maybe there will be some surprises from the Pluto-Kuiper Belt mission.

The mission found on July 14, 2015 that the planet had jagged landscapes around Pluto's equator that re made up of frozen methane.

Methane is a greenhouse gas and is relatively non-toxic. However this gas is extremely flammable and can explode. This gas limits the amount of oxygen that you can breathe as well.

The closest the space ship came was 7759 miles above Pluto's surface. The spaceship Horizon was traveling so fast it could not halt to spend time at Pluto. The mission was not planned to stop anywhere along the way.

The mission also discovered that the range of color on Pluto ranged from pale sections of off white and light blue, to streaks of yellow and subtle orange, to large patches of deep red.

Pluto may never be a planet again but it will always be noted in history that it once was.

Unlike Pluto the dog made famous by Walt Disney the little dwarf planet will hold the right to have been called a planet and then demoted. The dog will always be a cartoon dog.

12. EMMETT THE WOLF

Emmett was a grey wolf who lived in Yellowstone National Park. Let's start the story by telling you how Emmett's father met his mother. His father had traveled one thousand miles in search of a mate. Leaving Idaho and traveling to Wyoming to the Yellowstone National Park region. He traveled fifty miles a day for twenty days. Meeting Emmett's mother in Yellowstone where she had lived all her life.

She was roaming the valley looking for a mate. There was no one in her pack in which to mate with. So she left to start a pack with whatever mate she would find. It was a very lucky day when Emmett's father and mother met.

They met in a meadow where Emmett's father was fast asleep, weary from his travels. Emmett's father had killed an Elk and eaten about twenty two pounds of meat. Exhausted he laid down and had fallen asleep.

Emmett's mother came upon him, smelling him she could tell he was still breathing. His mother snored at the smell off Emmett's father. This woke his father.

They talked and walked around Yellowstone Park over several days. She showed him the hot springs, where to get fresh water and where to find game. During this time they decided to be mates.

His father had a narrow chest, his legs were long and closely set together at the front. When he ran his rear paws followed in the tracks of his front paws. He weighed eighty eight pounds, is thirty four inches at the shoulders and sixty three inches in length. His father's has a short torso and a long tail. His fur is mottled white, brown, grey and black with two thicknesses of fur. The top layer is for keeping him dry, the water just runs off. The next layer is the undercoating of fur which is a heavy down, this helps insulate him in the winter.

Emmett's mother has some of the same characteristics but she is smaller in size. She weighs eighty two pounds is shorter in length but her height, torso, tail and fur are much like his father's.

Emmett's parents are territorial which means they have staked out there hunting area and will protect it with their lives.

The pair travel as a family unit now. They will soon have pups, in about seventy five days Which will be in early April.

Until then they will hunt together finding deer and elk. They will hunt together which brings a good success rate.

In early April the pups are born. Emmett had four other siblings. They each weigh about one pound, their eyes and ears are closed.

Father will do all the hunting while mother takes care of the pups. Feeding them and keeping them warm.

Two weeks have passed since Emmett has been born. Now his eyes are starting to open and he is able to see some light. A few days and he will see fine. But, it will be another week before his ears open and he begins to hear.

Emmett and the other pups are always hungry and mother will nurse them for four weeks. Then she will start to wean them. Then she will teach them to eat meat.

One of Emmett's brother wandered from the den, he is killed by a mountain lion and several days later another pup is killed by a bear.

Only Emmett and his sister are left. Mother tells them not to wander from the den, that she must help father hunt now. Feeding two pups and two adults takes a lot of food.

The family is roaming the Yellowstone area. They are

traveling around thirty miles a day. They must move when the other game moves if they want to eat. Wolves require twenty two pounds of meat for a meal. The cubs eat less but still it requires a lot of hunting.

Emmett's teeth are all grown in now. He has forty two teeth with the power of fifteen hundred pounds of pressure when he bites down.

Emmett is learning all about his territory but there are hunters all around them. Humans are the most dangerous of all to the wolves because they kill for no reason at all other than to get the wolves fur. Our whole family is walking along a ridge which has very few trees. There is mostly just brush, then a shot rings out Kaboom! Kaboom! Kaboom! My sister falls to the ground and her body starts rolling down the mountain ridge. We run for our lives now trying to find cover.

Father says it is time to move out of this area and go up to a higher area. So we head for the Teton Mountains where father tells mother it will be safer.

Along our travels father will kill an Elk for our evening meal. Now it is time to get some rest. We have just bedded down for the night when on the edge of our camp we spot another lone wolf standing there.

Father goes over to him. The wolf says that he has no pack, that he is traveling alone. Father asks him if he wants to join us. The other wolf is younger than my father but older than me. The wolf decides that he will join us. My father and the wolf go off to talk and I fall fast asleep.

When we wake in the morning we will travel on towards the Teton Mountains. We are in the trees now, father and the other wolf have gone ahead scouting for food.

Mother keeps me moving along. Soon we come upon the others. They were looking down from the bluff they were sitting on. Below them was a grassy meadow near a spring running from the mountains side. Many Elk were grazing together or drinking from the spring.

Father tells us that we must circle around on both sides before we attack. The attack will take place at dusk. So we all sit and hear fathers plan for the attack.

Father takes me aside and tells me that I must go down slowly and be very quiet so the elks will not hear me. Stop take a break so you are not moving too fast. But, the most important thing is to calm yourself before the attack.

Emmett starts down the bluff on the right hand side, he is moving very slowly. He must watch where he places his paws so as not to step on a stick and break it. Emmett pauses as his heart is racing. This is his first real job as part of the pack. Emmett isn't sure he can do it, he's afraid.

Emmett is very nervous but he must keep going to his place for the attack. As he reaches his place, he lays down in wait for dusk to come. So he tries to calm himself like father had told him.

Dusk is about to come within minutes the attack will begin. Then it starts! They all spring towards the Elks, mother and father take down the first one. The new wolf and Emmett are still chasing their Elk. Then all of sudden they are bringing down their Elk. We will eat tonight thanks to the pack. This small hunt has made Emmett feel he is truly part of the pack now.

Many hunts and long miles they have traveled. The other wolf has been someone that Emmett could look up to. Emmett watched what the other wolf did and he would try to do the same thing. He has grown into a wolf who is now the size of his father.

Mother is going to have another litter of pups. Emmett wonders if it is time for him to move on by himself.

Emmett talks to the young wolf, he finds out his name is Ralph. Ralph tells him he felt the same but after he left the pack, he was sorry. Ralph knew he could not go back. Ralph roamed alone for a very long time and almost starved to death. He was close to being dead the night he found our camp. So he was very happy when Emmett's father asked him to join the pack. When your father offered me food, I was relieved that I wouldn't die. Ralph advised Emmett not to leave. The pack is the safest place you will ever have. You have protection with all of us around. Hunting alone isn't easy. It is the reason I almost starved to death. With the pack we hunt together making it easier bring down game. Besides you should stay to protect the new litter of pups.

So, Emmett stayed and he helped protect the pups. Watching over them so nothing would happen to them.

Ralph went looking for a mate. Found one wandering and lost. She had left her pack, going off to find a mate. So they became a pair.

The pack was growing and Emmett was becoming restless, he too wanted to find a mate.

One day on the mountain, sitting on and out cropping of rocks he saw way down in the meadow a lone wolf. The wolf looked injured but was coming his way. He decided to just sit and watch this wolf as it came towards him the wolf stumbled several times. Then all of a sudden the wolf just fell over hitting the ground hard. Emmett watched the wolf for a while wondering if he should approach this wolf.

Emmett decided to wander down to see if the wolf was dead. The wolf was breathing so Emmett just sat down next to it. He sat there for a while and then decided he would try talking to the wolf. The wolf didn't respond so he just kept talking. Finally he was hungry so

Emmett went to look for food. Telling the other wolf he would be back. Emmett didn't like leaving the wolf alone because if a bear came along, the bear would kill the wolf.

Emmett returned with some food but the wolf still didn't respond. Emmett laid down next to the wolf and fell asleep.

Sometime during the night Emmett heard the other wolf stirring so he sat up. Emmett asked the wolf if he was all right. The wolf tells Emmett that she is a girl that her family had been killed by a bear. That she had been traveling for more than twenty days but had only been able to hunt a few rabbits. She said that she was very weak and also that she was hungry.

Emmett knew that the deer he killed for his supper still had some meat left on it. So off Emmett went to fetch some for her. Carrying the meat back between his teeth, he placed it at her feet. She ate very slowly having a hard time to chew because she was so weak. Her strength was coming back to her. She finished all of the meat he had brought. Emmett then told her to rest that he would take her to his pack in the morning.

The morning sun rose in the west, they ate some more of the deer meat. Then they were headed to see the rest of the pack. The pack excepted her story, telling her she could join their pack if she wished to.

Fall is here the snow is falling on the mountain range

telling the animals it is time to travel to the valley below. The migration to the valley has started, all the game is going down to the valley where they will be shelter some from the long winter ahead. There are the warm springs in the valley that will help to keep the animals warm during the deep snow falls. The buffalo, deer and elk will paw at the ground for grass. The noise that make will drive the rabbit from the ground for easy hunting. Survival of all the animals was hard fought during the winter months.

Winter came and went. The pack had survived another winter. The hunting had been good and the cold not so bad this year. The pack was healthy and everyone was in good shape with no injuries. Ralph and his mate announced that they were going to have a litter of pups. That meant the pack was growing again, it was a happy time for the pack.

Emmett had finally got up the courage to ask the female wolf to be his mate. She said she would but he had to agree to one thing. Emmett asked what that one thing was. The she wolf told him he would have to agree to always stay with this pack because it was the only family she knew now.

So they are a pair now, mated for life. They didn't know what would come in the future. But they knew that they would always be together. Always be part of the pack.

13. LANDON'S ADVENTURE

In 1859 Landon was a young man, single with no children. He lived with his parents on the East coast of the United States.

Landon was born in a small town in northeastern Connecticut. He grew up hunting and fishing with his father. He loved to camp on the islands of the Quinebaug River with his uncle.

Landon like all young men was seeking adventure. He had heard of the gold in the west that was free for the digging. He thought he would go and get rich then come back home a wealthy man.

There was talk all over town of a wagon train leaving for the west. So Landon went in search of the wagon master hoping to secure a place on the wagon train. When he found the wagon master he was told there was one spot left and whoever paid for that spot would be going. Landon reached into his pocket and pulled out the money. He paid the wagon master so he was sure he had a spot.

Now he must secure a wagon with the money he had left. It wouldn't leave him much money for the trip but he figured he would be all right.

Having secured his wagon he began to pack it with all his worldly possessions which wasn't much. He had his clothes, rifle, hunting knife and his fishing pole. Along with the bedding and blankets his mother had supplied. Along with some money she had given him, telling him to save it in case he needed to come home.

Landon's family wished him well as the wagon train was getting ready to leave. They were there to send him off on his adventure. His father told him to stay safe and hurry back home to them. His mother cried and handed him her Bible telling him you may need this for comfort on your long journey.

Landon was off on his adventure with a very limited amount of food supplies. It was all right because he wasn't much of a cook anyway. He would hunt for his food on the trip because he knew how to cook meat. Little did he know how far he was about to travel and how long it would take them to get there.

Landon and the others on the wagon train had no idea that they were about to travel one thousand nine hundred and fifty miles. Or that the journey would take them at least six months to get where they were going. Traveling conditions were very hard, long hours and many problems along the way.

Wagon wheels would fell off and have to be put back on which required others to help lift the wagon and sometimes the wagons would have to be unloaded to be able to do this. Wagons got stuck in the mud and would have to be pushed to get the going again. There were rivers to cross. Crossing rivers was probably the hardest thing because the river would have to be scouted to find the safest place to cross and still there were other obstacles like fast running water or the river was higher than they expected. Wagons would still get stuck on rocks or in holes that couldn't be seen. Then the wagon would have to be pushed or pulled out of the river to free them. People couldn't swim so lines would need to be set up for them to hold on to, still some people drown. These things all slowed the wagon train down.

So many people also walked because there wasn't room in the wagons to carry them. Landon liked to help the youngsters so he would carry as many in his wagon as he could because he had fewer possessions then others on the wagon train.

There was sickness among the people on the wagon train because of the heat, lack of food or water.

Two months into the traveling food was becoming scares. People had not realized how much food they would need or how long the trip would be. They ate well the first month having used more than they needed to. So know they would have to stop the wagon train to get food for everyone. Half of the men went fishing and the other half went hunting. Landon would have liked to have gone fishing but they left that for the older men.

The women would make some stick frames to dry the fish and game that the men brought back. This would be shared by everyone on the wagon train. They also needed to seek out a place to get fresh water. They preferred a spring that was running. Bad water would make everyone sick on the train. They stored the water in big barrels that were stored on the side of the wagons.

Landon shared his water because his o fill the barrel was pretty full, there was only him and his horses. So he was willing to share with others that might be running low. But he to know needed water so they went off up the stream looking for a place to fill the barrels.

They found a large water fall about a mile upstream where they would be able to fill the barrels. The decision was made that they would travel there as soon as they had enough food.

In the mean time they would take water from the stream and boil it so that no one would get sick. This water would be kept separate so as not to contaminate the barrels. The horses could drink from the stream south of where they were camping. These were only a few of their struggles, many had blisters on their feet and had a hard time walking, which slowed the wagon train.

Finally they reached a small town, some of the people were going to stay because they were too sick to go farther or just couldn't go on. Landon decide to stay also.

Landon heard about the gold and silver that had been found of Pike's Peak and decided he would go up on the mountain and work in the mine. He still had the money his parents had given him. There had been no where to spend it on the trail. So Landon decided he would hold on to like is mother had said to do.

Landon went up the mountain to work in the mine.
He would be paid ten dollars for six days of work often
working ten hours a day. The first week was the worst,
he was sick but the other men told him he would be all
right once his body got use to having less oxygen.
Because of the height of the mountain there was less
oxygen.

Landon found the mine so poorly lit which was causes
by less oxygen. The candles wouldn't stay lit in the
mine. It was hot and the smell of the others men's sweat
made him feel ill. The working conditions were very
dangerous. Men fell off from ladders because of the
angle that they were placed on. Some of the men got sick
from drinking the dirty water that was provided the
miners in pails that were uncovered. Dust fell into the
pail from the work the miners did. The miners didn't
know that the water would make them sick, they fell that
the company provided it so it was all right to drink.

Landon slipped on some lose rock and fell breaking
his leg. Landon had to be carried down the mountain as
they had no doctor up at the mines. Landon would be out
of work for six weeks and probably longer.

Landon was distressed that this would cause him to
loss all the money he had saved. But it was his lucky
day. The doctor that they took him to was one of the
people he had traveled with on the wagon train.

Landon had saved his two twin boys from drowning

on the trip west. The doctor who they had nicknamed on the trip was called Doc. Doc told Landon he could stay with them at no cost till he was well again.

The two boys George and Will were very happy about this arrangement. Their mother tried to keep them from bothering Landon but the boys would sneak in to see him any change they got. They loved to talk to Landon about what mining was like. Also, they liked to hear about his fishing tales and the tales about hunting they thought were a little wild but they liked hearing them anyway.

Landon and Doc would talk late into the night about mining and the conditions the miners worked under. Doc was very interested as he treated many of the miners sometimes it was too late to help them.

Landon and Doc talked about the falls off ladders because of the angles they were placed on. How slipping on rocks like he had were often because the rocks were left on the floor of the mines scattered all about. Landon told him of how many of the men suffered from some kind of poisoning.

Doc was telling Landon it was probably mercury, lead or arsenic poisoning. There was no way to be sure. Because so many of the miners had other health problems. Doc told Landon that not having fresh water also contributed to all the health problems they had.

Landon told Doc that mining was very dangerous. Men would put up shoring to support the walls and ceiling but they weren't sure how it was suppose to be done.

The men setting the dynamite weren't always careful about blowing up things or how much dynamite to use this was endangering the miners. Just the dust from the blasting was a problem the men were inhaling all this dust. Landon felt many of these issues had to be addressed or the miners would keep dying very young.

Miners were now being forced to purchase a license which cost them thirty shillings a month. This money was supposed to cover maintaining the police force in the goldfields. It wasn't enough money to cover maintaining the police force. The miners rebelled and stopped paying for the license.

Landon was getting better and starting to walk on his own. Doc didn't think it was a good idea that he went back to mining so Doc came up with an idea. Doc thought would be a good idea if Landon opened a shop in town. Doc told Landon that he had folks back East that could help him to purchase items to sell.

Landon thought maybe it was a good idea but he had never been a business man. He didn't have a lot of money to get started. If he did this his father could make money too. But how was he going to do this.

Doc told him that he would be his business partner and he would help put up the money to get started. Doc told him he had some other ideas too.

Landon told Doc that he was very young with no

experience at all and what happened if he failed. Doc told him you won't fail because you know more about business than you think.

Landon started to tell Doc about the clothes the miners wore and the tools they used. The kind of food supplies they had when he was up on the mountain.

Landon told Doc about the Levi jeans and loose fitting trousers they wore. How most of the miners wore loose fitting shirts and how they all needed sturdy mining boots.

Doc wanted Landon to tell him about the tools the miners used. Landon told him that they needed picks, axes, shovels and picks but they had to be sturdy and hold up.

Doc tells Landon see you know all about what is going to be needed in your store. You know what you want and we will work the rest of it out. All you have to do know is make a list and OH! By the way you own the store next door all you have to is clean it up. There is a place for you to sleep in the upstairs of the building.

Landon remember why you are doing this to improve the miners lives. We have one thousand people in this town and only one store. That store is able to charge anything they want and people have to pay it or go without. Bye the way don't forget to order tents and bedrolls.

Landon tells Doc I will not cheat the people I will ask

a decent price for a good product. I will sell to make a profit but not to get rich or charge more for a product that isn't worth buying. I have seen enough of that from the other store owner.

Doc tells Landon that he needs to remember that we have women in this town and they have needs. I am sure my wife will help you with that. The boys will help you clean up the store I am sure of that.

The store is very dirt and it has a lot of junk in it but we are partners so we will all help.

George, Will and Mary, Doc's wife came early the next day. They brought pails, rags, mops and a broom. Mary told Landon and the boys to get to work and clean out the broken furniture.

The boys started helping Landon remove all the broken furniture out that couldn't be repaired. They started piling it out back by the shed. When an old man comes out of the shed the boys jump back. Landon asked the man why was he in he shed. The man told him that he had nowhere to sleep, that he had been working in the mine till he couldn't breathe up there on the mountain. Landon felt sorry for him and told him that he could sleep in the shed as long as he didn't have any fire.

Landon and the boys go back inside to finish what they had started. Will came rushing in to tell Landon that he had to come and see what he saw with his own eyes.

Landon couldn't imagine what had happened now. So

George, Will and Landon went outside to see what was happening. There before their eyes the old man was repairing the furniture that they had brought out.

Landon wanted to know what the man's name was. The man stated that his name was Harry he had learned to make furniture back east. Harry told them he had a business in Boston but he gave it up to chase gold.

Landon made a deal with Harry that if he would help him get the store up and running that he would let him repair or build furniture in the storage room. If he repaired the furniture he would give him a room upstairs over the store. Harry thought that was a great idea.

Later that night Harry, Landon and Doc sat around the potbelly stove drinking coffee talking about what had happened that day. Doc stated that they now would all be partners. They all laughed and stated that yes we are.

Doc reminded Landon what a god man he was. I am sure you will be a fair and honest business man. He was sure that Landon would never take advantage of anyone in this town.

Doc told Landon that if he wanted to get supplies soon that there was a wagon train coming with supplies. The first one to make a fair and honest deal with the wagon master would get the supplies. So if you are interested we need to ride now.

Landon and Doc saddled up and rode into the night. They rode all day until finally they came upon the wagon train that was just stopping in a meadow near a river bank.

Doc had told Landon that the wagon master would give him a good and fair price. I know that the other store in town marks up the prices three times what he pays for them. That is why I wanted you to intercept the wagon train before it got to town.

The wagon master wanted to know what they were doing on the road at this time of night. Landon and Doc explained that they wanted to do business with him. The wagon master name was Jake. Jake told them to have supper with them but he would not talk business until after supper. They all sat down to eat around the open campfire. They sat talking about the trip they had made. Jake told them he made this trip twice a year.

When supper was over they sat around the campfire as the other men retired to bed for the night. Jake told Landon he would be happy to do business with him if they could agree on a price. Jake told them that the man in town owed him money for the last delivery. Jake told them it was important to him that his men got paid. He could go without but his men had to be paid they had families and supplies to pay for.

Jake and Landon came to an agreement on how much money it would be for the supplies. Landon was happy that Jake had showed him what he had brought for the other store and the price was all right. They talked about future deliveries and how Landon's father would be involved in the ordering.

They agreed upon two trips a year. Money would be paid ahead of the delivery. They shook hands on the deal. Landon and Jake exchanged money that they had agreed upon. Jake thanked Landon for his honesty and fair trading.

Landon, Jake and Doc retired for the night. Jake told them they would leave early in the morning.

The sun was coming up, it was early dawn, the mist was still rising from the river. Rabbits were in the meadow eating. Landon was stiffing the air and smelled the bacon sizzling over the open fire. The bacon was wafting through the air, it was like being pulled by the nose to where the bacon was cooking. Landon's stomach ached with hunger as he strolled towards the campfire. Landon was surprised to find Doc cooking the bacon and eggs.

Landon told Doc I didn't think you could cook. Doc told Landon that he had to eat before he was married. Landon told Doc that his mother had cooked for him and when he was with the wagon train some of the women cooked for him. Landon told Doc that he guessed he had been a lucky man.

They all sat down to enjoy the bacon and eggs and talk about the rest of the trip. Jake told them he would handle things when they got to town, you and the boys unload your supplies while I handle business.

I'll let him know that we are done doing business and

get the money that is owed me.

They rode into town and started to unload. George and Will came to help which made the job go twice as fast.

Jake had gone to settle his business with the other store keeper. It didn't go well. Jake wasn't looking for any problems, he knew the other man was probably upset that he had already sold the supplies. Jake need the money that the man owed him.

The other man was refusing to pay him. Jake told him that he wanted no hard feelings just what he had coming to him.

Jake told the man if he wouldn't give him the money he wanted his merchandise. The man told him he was getting neither. Jake told him he would get the sheriff if he had to. The man told him to do whatever he had to.

Jake told the man once more that if he wouldn't give him the money he would go to the sheriff. He would have the sheriff come to the store while he removed his merchandise.

The man told him he could do whatever he wants to do. So, Jake went over to the sheriff's office. Jake explained to the sheriff what had happened and about the man's refusal to pay him. Jake told the sheriff all I want is my money or my merchandise. The sheriff agreed with Jake.

Jake and the sheriff walked back over to the man's store.

Landon saw Jake walking with the sheriff and was concerned that something was wrong. He didn't want Jake to have any trouble with the store owner. Landon found the sheriff telling the man that he had to pay or let Jake have his merchandise.

The man decided he would pay Jake the money he owed. He told Jake you better watch out. The sheriff asked him if he was threatening Jake because if he was he would have to take him to jail.

Jake told the man that he wasn't looking for trouble but he would never do business with him again.

Landon, Jake and the sheriff went over to Landon's store for a cup of coffee. They sat talking about Landon opening the store.

Landon talked about Harry fixing all the furniture. What a help he had been to him. The sheriff told Landon that he was very glad to hear that. The sheriff told Landon that he had been afraid that he would have to steal to eat and that he would have to put him in jail.

Landon told the sheriff that he was living with him upstairs and doing all the cooking. The sheriff was happy to hear this.

Many months go by, business is good. People in town are very happy with the way the store is run and the fair prices. Landon had written his father and now he was taking care of ordering.

During the winter months Harry had been building and repairing furniture. Landon had been selling it in the store and Harry had made enough money to start his own wood shop. There was a store on the other side of Doc's office. The building had been abandoned and the town was willing to give it to him for his business. Harry was not a rich miner but rich in his own way.

It has been a long winter but they had brought the telegraph in just before the snow started to fall in the mountains. I sent my first telegraph around Christmas. I remembered that my mother loved Christmas.

Soon Spring would come. The town had grown up but the mines were starting to close they had become dangerous and the gold had run out. I was due to get a shipment soon and I will enjoy seeing Jake again.

Spring has arrived the birds were returning, the snow was leaving the mountain. The streams were running much faster because of the melt on the mountains. This has Landon, Harry, George, Will, Doc and the sheriff spring fever. They all decided to go fishing. Mary had packed a big lunch to feed them all, so they grabbed their fishing poles and hiked to a stream across the meadow.

The day was a real warm spring day with the sun beating down on them while they were fishing. They fished till noon before they stopped to eat under the Oak trees by the stream. When lunch was over the boys went back to fishing. The men laid under the oak tree to take a nap.

Soon the boys became bored with fishing and decided they would go swimming. The boys jumped into the water sending water splashing up on the men who were taking a nap on the bank of the stream.

Landon woke first, yanking off his boots and shirt he jumped into the stream. Soon all the others joined them. Splashing each other and dunking one another. They were laughing and having a good time. The sun was going down and know it was time to hike back home. They all walked home laughing, they didn't have any fish but it was a great day of fun.

They were walking into town as they spotted the wagon train in front of Landon's store. They ran towards the store know everyone was excited to see Jake.

Landon drew close he couldn't belief his eyes there was his mother and father standing in front of his store talking to Mary.

Landon's mother told him that they had come to be a family again. Landon asked her what about the ordering. She told him that there is a telegraph. Everything is set-up with Jake.

Landon tells all of them that he had come to get rich, instead I found partners, two boys that treat me like I am their brother and a town that I love. Now my family is here. I would say I am a rich man for not having found any gold.

Landon became very wealthy selling Levi jeans and other supplies. He later married and had several children.

Yes, Levi jeans went on the market in 1853 and we are still wearing them today.

14. BENJAMIN BEAVER

Benjamin beaver was a well dressed beaver. He wore a top hat and a long black coat. He walked around the town with his cane during the late afternoon. Many of the animals in town thought he was just strutting around to show off.

Beaver had a bushy white tail and long sleek body. He weighed about fifty five pounds and only worked at night. He had ten people in his family but they weren't show offs like Benjamin was.

Benjamin told anyone who would listen that he was the best looking animal in town. Ben told everyone that they couldn't stand in his shadow let alone compete with his looks.

Ben wasn't able to see very well but he was to proud to wear his glasses, so at times he stumbled over things falling to the ground.

The animals would laugh and ask him if his tail was too heavy for him to carry it. This made Ben very mad.

The animals all made fun of Ben because they said that he was to proud and his tail was no better than anyone else's.

Owl tried to tell Ben not to brag so much that it hurt the other animals feeling. But, Ben just couldn't stop bragging about his tail.

Ben felt that the other animals needed to learn to respect him. Ben thought that he deserved it because he was a great builder of dams, which gave them all water year round.

Ben knew he had sharp teeth as he cut down the aspen and poplar trees. He used these to build his dam at night. That was the best time to work, when no one was around.

Mrs. Goose came walking by and Ben wanted her to look at his tail. The goose told him it was no prettier than hers. This made been become very irate. Ben told the Mrs. Goose that he could stay underwater for fifteen minutes or more, can you? Mrs. Goose walked on ignoring what Ben was saying.

Ben told Owl I have a beautiful home with a room for just drying my tail. Another beautiful room for my family.

Owl told Ben you are looking for trouble with the other animals. You need to learn to act like the other animals for they are not prideful.

Owl told Ben they had sent for Coyote to come. Coyote was a trickster and a predator of beaver.

Ben thought and thought about what to do. So, he went home to clean his tail and brush out all the mud from his tail. Then he would walk down main street and show all the animals how beautiful his tail was.

Later that day Ben strolled down the street to show all the animals his magnificent tail. The dark fur was shiny and bright. It was a nice tail but so was squirrels and foxes. But all his trip down main street got was more laughter and nasty remarks about his tail.

That was the final straw for Benjamin Beaver he would show them all. He had decided to flood the whole town. Then they would show him some respect.

Ben went to work cutting down Willow, Black Cherry and maple trees. He worked all day in the hot sun. Ben worked so hard that he didn't notice his tail was getting full of mud and other small sticks.

Night came and Ben was hard at work building first one dam and then the next. This would take several days to build four dams.

All he could think of was how sorry the animals would be when he flooded their homes and they would have to move.

What he hadn't thought of was that then he would be all alone.

The building went on for several nights. Ben was looking at the moon which had a bright light around it, with a orange ring around that but it was covered with a mist in front of it. Ben thought this is a bad omen, I must stop building for the night.

So, Ben went back to cutting down more trees. He was working on this big Oak tree which would take a long time to bring it down. He kept working at it and all of a sudden the tree fell landing right on his beautiful tail.

Ben worked for hours trying to free himself from the tree. Exhausted he collapsed on the ground and fell asleep. He dreamed of walking down main street and all the animals clapping, cheering and hollering at him about his beautiful tail.

Ben woke up only to find that his beautiful tail was still stuck under the tree. His tail was swollen and aching. So Ben decided that he had to get his tail out or it would never be beautiful again.

Ben started to dig down in the mud along the banking of the pond. He dug for what seemed forever. His back ached from having to twist around to dig. Finally success his tail was free. The tail was so swollen that it ached. Ben swam to the coldest part of the pond to see if he could reduce the swelling.

The swelling went down but Ben could not believe what he saw. His beautiful, beautiful tail was flat.

Ben slapped his tail on the water trying to make his beautiful tail come back. The other animal told him that his tail was no longer beautiful because he was being punished for bullying the other animal. .Ben thought back to the night he had looked up at the moon. He knew then it was an omen but not the one he thought.

So you see when a beaver is pounding his tail

on the water it is because he is in distress. The beaver no longer has a beautiful tail or maybe he does. It's all in how you look at things.

15. THE CLASSROOM

This is a story written by one of the students I had in Learning in Retirement. The challenge when they come in is to write how they felt when entering the building for the writing class.

The day had started and as I ventured forth towards a new chapter in life. Although it was still early in the day I found myself amidst unfamiliar surroundings. Eagerly I pressed on towards something I thought I had left behind years before. If memory serves me right and "History does repeat herself" then "Surprise!!! I was going back to school.

As I meandered down the hallway I focused my gaze intently from going left to right and then back again to my left. I felt enthusiasm mixed with apprehension as I was eagerly seeking the door to my assigned classroom. Pressing on into the unknown I moved quietly down the hallway, inch by inch, step by step. I was becoming aware that something was amiss. Something was not the way I had remembered it.

Although over the years time has afforded me a reasonable amount of knowledge, wisdom, and understanding, it has also robbed me of the tenacity so often found in youthful independence. With hunching shoulders and limping leg I repulsively ignores the slowing cantor of my new wavering and wobbly stride. "The die is cast", "Can't turn back now", thus determination spurred me on.

Arriving at school early I expected to find that the wasted strength of youth had returned to me. I had hopes that the proverbial "Second wind: I had heard ao much about was waiting to kick in. but somehow the comfort found in familiar sights and sounds of yesteryear were noticeably missing "Shoot" I was relying on these to resurface and come to my rescue thus encouraging my endeavor. In a panic struck moment I questioned if I was in the right place. Fear, entwining her cold arms around my heart tried to encourage me to go back home and get more sleep over this.

I know times change and progress waits for no man. However, I was hoping to be greeted with at least a little bit of friendly archaic nostalgia. After all, isn't school still school? I thought, "How wonderful the feeling would be to bring back, if only for a moment, the impulsive and carefree days of yore." Learning was never something I had opted for. My goal then as it will always be is to use the gathering of knowledge as a vehicle for having fun.

Purposely I propelled myself further into the labyrinth of hallways and corridors. I simply took to enjoying each individual moment of searching and listening for familiar things. All of a sudden and without warning it began to happening. The fading memories painted across the canvas of my mind began taking shape. Deep in thought and plausible expectations, I had stepped into the "Twilight Zone."

While gingerly treading down the corridor with my head in a cloud of anticipation I began tilting my "Word Catchers" to the left for a better chance of hearing. My right profile is truly my best side but my hearing is audibly enhanced when turning to the left.

What was going on? I thought I heard echoing in my ears the click, click, click, from taps we used to wear on our shoes. Coming to my senses I became a little bit saddened thinking "The use of a hearing aid is getting closer." I discarded this thought almost immediately when looking down and seeing the multicolored carpet beneath my feet. It was only my desire for reliving the past translating me but for a second or two back into the twilight zone.

The walls, were adorned with posters and corkboards that were definitely informative as one passed by. However, their presence seemed to lack the old school charm found in the long line of grey lockers that were surely a between class necessity for adolescent socializing.

On my right I saw a classroom with A131

written on it. Finally, I had arrived at my destination. Relieved for the moment I stopped and looked straight ahead. Then taking a deep breath, I reached out for the satin silver doorknob just inches away. Apprehensively I placed my shaking hand on the door and immediately I felt once again being tossed between two different time zones. "It's not possible" I thought for this to be real. This wooden door in front of me is exactly the same size and color that English 101 used to be in High School. Then, looking closer my chin dropped in utter astonishment. Perplexed I silently whispered to my disbelief, "It also has the same little, eye level, square window, right in the middle.

I paused, took a deep breath, and asked myself, "Would it be wise for me to enter in?" curiosity got the best of me and so using caution I opened the door and walked into the empty classroom. I was early but that's a good thing. I remembered that back in the days being late would have had tongues wagging. At least that's what I remember DO ME DOTTIE always used to say trying to warn us something only the girls seem to understand. Now confident that I was not going to be attacked or sucked into some other dimension for all eternity I looked around, chose a desk in the middle of the room and sat down. Satisfied at my decisiveness I sighed, "Wow! I'm back in school." However, after looking around and assessing my surroundings I became partially disappointed. Nothings sacred anymore I thought realizing times had really changed

The space around the walls close to the ceiling that used to display the alphabet in both upper and lower cases were missing. Also missing at the front of each individual desk was an inkwell. This ancient artifact was kept empty. It wasn't filled with ink until after a student produced proficiency in pencil penmanship thus earning a Rite of Passage into the world of literacy. Then a black stylus and a metal pen tip was the sign of scholarly accomplishments. I believe it was during the year 1950 that we received our first ball point pens. The inkwell still holds many a fond memory for a boy who always found solace engaging in aeronautical experiments with paper airplanes and psychological inkblot interpretations.

While sitting there enjoying my reverie and with my eyes closed I remembered the orange juice we received for morning recess and the half pint of milk we received during the afternoon. I can almost taste the sweet flavor of un-homogenized milk. This was a farm fresh milk that would naturally separate the milk from the cream if left standing. This raw milk had a unique flavor that has been sadly lost to the world today through progress.

I was brought back to the present as I heard someone entering the room. It was my teacher. Even this meeting between teacher and student has over the years changed. I remember back then that when standing next to my teacher I looked young enough to be the teacher's son. Today's encounter found the teacher looking young enough to be my daughter.

Time marches on for each generation with its victories and defeats. However, this old man with a profound quest for getting knowledge, wisdom, and understanding knows he must keep in step with the present and alls its technology. This is truly a necessity if expecting to embrace the joys that a full and exciting life still has to offer. Yet, the days of one room, two grade school houses, walking to school instead of riding a bus, brown bag lunches instead of cafeterias, pencils and paper instead of smart phones and tablet, decorating for dances in the gym, and getting to experience Sadie Hawkins Day still remain fondest memories of my youth. It has been an honor to have lived them then and now, a privilege in choosing to keep the best alive as I remember how they used to be

Even procuring an "A" with the proverbial apple for the teacher has changed to a large "Hot chocolate with whipped cream."

Written by Len Watson

I only have a few things to add here the first

being I am not a teacher, I introduced writing to people because I think it is a health skill to have. It also helps us remember both the present and the pass. I appreciated each person that came to my writing class. They all brought their own uniqueness and different styles.

So take up your pens and start writing, you don't have to show it to anyone but some day you may chose to share it with the world. Oh! I can't write. That is an old line everyone learned to write sentences so get started on your journey and "Just Keep Writing."

ABOUT THE AUTHOR

I enjoy writing very much it is a hobby of mine. I have been writing for many years. I have encouraged others to write. I live in Eastern, Connecticut.